You're A Redflag And That's Ok!

Rjay Verdida

Ukiyoto Publishing

Dedication

If this book is really passed the evaluation and published. I will thank the Lord and Him alone because of his goodness and greatness.

Also to; Krizzilyn, John Mark, Kimberly, Allysa, Juliana, Ate Jana, Kuya Arby, Ate Emy, Kuya Devs, Angelo John Pedrie, Cesa, and Shania Shayne. Thank you everyone for believing in me while the crowd did not. Love lots!

Contents

Overthinking   1

Scared of the Past   5

Attachment Issue   9

Relationship Grabber   12

Dictator   16

Impulsive Decision Maker   20

Overload Expectation   24

Untamed Jealousy   27

Insensitive   31

Too Much Asking For Validation   34

One Sided POV   37

Silent Treatment Issue   40

Mix Signals Aren't Healthy   43

About the Author   *48*

Overthinking

"OVERTHINKING ends up becoming a heavy baggage"

Being an overthinker is a red flag. And that is ok!

I know. Some of you will ask themselves, "Why being an overthinker is a red flag? We are supposed to be the victims of toxic relationships and heart aches! Why is this book attacking us?! I'm overthinking! I can't read this book anymore. It is bad for my mental health. I must close this now!"

Ok wait. Calm down little one. Before you close this book. Did you ask yourself before why you are always overthinking things? Why can't your mind find solace no matter how you try?

Did you ask yourself before what's wrong in you and why your mind doesn't stop overthinking what if's, buts, should I's, and Could I's?

Did you really ask yourself why are you like that? A walking-living-time-bomb for every beings near you that who ever touch the little trigger of your anxiety, you will explode?

Do you really ask yourself why you are an overthinker? Or you just 'always' blaming the beings that triggered you?

Yes? Or no?

We stand to the answer 'no'. Because you are still continuing reading this book to find the answer to why you are made up like that.

Maybe you're right. Maybe you are like that because of overloaded problems, family crisis, financial dilemma, study peer-pressures, toxic-past-relationships, or whatever our world can offer.

Maybe you are right. You are like that because of them. And cursed them from molding you like that. Cursed them for changing your innocent soul from being a walking-time-bomb.

But remember this young one, It is ok.

It is ok to be an overthinker. It is ok that your red flag is being worried about everything.

Butt honey… it is not ok if you try to sit comfortably on that throne. You must exiled yourself in that phase and move forward. Do not normalize being an overthinker.

Do not take the comfort of your comfort zone. Because if you do that, you mess up everything later.

You will probably fail to achieve everything you want because you will worry too much about the pros and cons of your actions. And oftentimes, it will lead you to not giving a try to a thing you desire because you're scared of the result. You will always ask yourself, "What could have been?"

And especially, you will fail to be a good partner. Because you will worry too much about your relationship. You will blame your partner for his wrong doings. You will be a self centered partner and only see your agony but not your partner's side trying so hard to understand and be with you.

Maybe yes. Maybe the quote, "If you don't want your partner to overthink. Give him/her the assurance she/he wanted and the whole truth," is correct. But young one, are we always guaranteed to ourselves that if our partner gives us assurance and the naked truth in us, our mind will stop to think of other problems and what if's?

No. Because our mind is a restless system. It will always think of possibilities and outcomes, that can lead you to get anxious and make impulsive decisions inside the relationship that both of you, your partner, are in, that will cause severe wounds for both of you.

And we don't want that to happen. We don't want you to hurt the being you love because your mind speaks louder than your soul. And for that to avoid. You must tame your demons in your head first.

You must invest more love in yourself. To your mind. Tamed your restless mind. Embrace it with your self love. Pour it with assurance, consistency, and perseverance that you deserve and crave.

Don't wait for others to do that job for you because you are not a freaking damsel in distress that is trapped into a 20-feet above the ground tower with a huge dragon as a guard.

Be an independent young one!

You don't need a knight, Mr. Green flag, or even a mind reader partner to restrain your own demon. The only person you need to keep your demons in your head quite is you.

Invest more on your peace of mind. Do what makes your soul happy. Go to church, re-read your favorite novels, hang out with friends, date yourself, anything. Do the thing that makes you calm and valid.

Practice your mind to stop worrying about what people think about you, stop expecting too much in a given situation, stop thinking about the future always, and stop hoping for what if's and possibility so your mind can rest.

And most importantly, eat what present offers you to eat. Sometimes, because we worry too much, we forget that we are still living in the present.

We always hang up our neck to the future waiting for the outcome that results from our false-expectations. We always try so hard to look above the walls that we forget to look where our feet are rooted.

Future is important but always remember that the present is much more important because what you do in the present is what you will be in the future.

Practice on how to strive hard in the present rather than to think about the future. Play blind about your worries. Do not fret about what the future holds and always try to step forward.

Practice that and always safeguard your peace of mind. Make that as your habit. Forget the conclusion that for you to find your solace, you need someone that really understands you.

No. Understand yourself first. Don't rely on other beings to fix you. Fix your unstable mind on your own. Be an empowered and independent soul who does not need a superman just to be saved in their darkest days.

Build your own empire using your own tears, hardships, sufferings, and broken heart pieces. Show to the world what he did to you. What traumatizing past experiences did to your innocent soul and pass them with grace like a Victoria's Secret model.

Do not let traumatizing experiences of your past stop you from being a better person. Learn the art of moving on and make it a habit that what is past is past. Maybe that past changed you in a way, but always remember, human beings are a walking living-progress. As we grow, we bloom and evolve more beautifully than yesterday. Your growth wont stop there.

That is just a start.

Be your own savior. Be your own superman. Be your own home, young one. Live.

Scared of the Past

"NOTHING in life is to be feared; it is only to be understood." - Marie Curie

Being scared of the past is a red flag. But it is ok!

We can't help but be scared about our past. Especially when our past gives us the trauma we still carry today. And it is ok. I understand that you are just scared that it might happen again to you. That's why you always try to compare the changes in your life to your past so you can avoid it as soon as possible if you see similarities.

But honey, remember. You can't move forward willingly if you are still stuck in your trauma. In your past.

I know this might look like an insensitive attack on your soft spot, but, what I am trying to show you is the beauty of life served in front of you, that you have already forgotten to look at because you are busy looking at your back. Worrying always if someone will try to stab you with the same trauma you already carried.

You can't move forward like that, young one. You can't. Because you will not see what the world can still offer to you if you are afraid to even look at the glimpse of your future without it.

So what if the same trauma will surface again if you try to move forward? What if this time, you might hurt yourself badly for risking again? What if you bleed badly because you try to live again? And what if the wound that it caused did not heal this time?

Do we really need to mend the wounds our trauma's always leaving us?

No. We don't need to. We have the right to keep those. To Leave it like that and walk with grace and heads held high with everyone. Showing the world our flaws and bruises.

It is our sign of survival. It is the sign that we survive in the hardship of life. Live with it and make it your reference to choose better decisions in the future.

We can't deny the fact that the past gave us heavy baggage and trauma. That is why we are so scared because of the past. But always remember that if you lock yourself in that phase in your life, and someone enters your life with great intention to love you…

You will just hurt that being because you can't reciprocate the same energy and love that being gives you because you are so freaking busy trying to compare that being in your past trauma.

You can't let that being live in your heart if someone's memory is still there. You will just hurt that pure soul for trying to reciprocate his feelings while also trying to live in your past.

You can't multitask things. Especially when you're trying to live in your present while your soul is still intact in your past.

You need to choose how you want to live. And you must always choose to live in the present. Always choose to move forward even though it hurts badly every step and you think you can't already.

Always choose yourself more than living with your trauma. Because sometimes, we are too busy meddling in our broken hearts that we forget that in everything that is happening to us; there is a reason.

It always has and we will just realize it when we reach that moment in our life that we are no longer in the dark of our past.

So live young one.

Walk out in the dark zone of your past. Don't live there. It is intoxicating. Walk in the light. See what world unfolds to you. Eat what the world can offer every day.

Learn to dance with the waves of life. Come what may it is. You can surpass all of it. You have your family, friends, and Him in your back. Don't fret.

Don't be scared to fail. Because if you did, cry out loud. It is ok. Your feelings are valid. Release your resentment at how life is freaking so unfair and after that, go, stand again and be a better version of yourself than the previous one.

Take the lesson and leave the bad experiences and memories behind. Don't let the past mold you for being your better version. Let the lesson do its job to complete your being. Take your time to heal and don't settle until you completely build your own home in yourself.

So if ever the time has come, and someone will come into your life with great intention of loving you—you can love that being to the fullest without comparing, resonating, and worrying about your past.

You can genuinely be happy by that time because finally, you make yourself a nomad that doesn't get stuck in one place.

You make yourself your home that's why whenever someone will leave you. You understood the drill. You don't beg that person to stay. Hence. You will let that being go and experience something with someone else with a grateful though heavy heart.

But at least, at the end of the day, you still have yourself and your heart together with the lesson that person leaves you and the happy memories you both make together. And those moments will be your forever, nostalgia. Together with the other memories you make with other people from your past.

So you see, life is beautiful if you look at it with an optimistic perspective.

You try, you fail, you get stuck, you realize, you heal, you try again, you fail again, you heal again, you try again, but fail again. But try again, and succeed.

Life really sucks sometimes or… 'often'. But, the process you have to get through to realize it is wonderful and beautiful. You just have to understand life itself to see things from a different set point.

So yeah honey, it is ok. It is ok to be scared of the past.

You might hurt someone who had genuine affection for you in the past because of that red flag of yours. But always remember, it is ok.

It is part of life we must understand. It is part of your progress to be a better version of yourself. And I know, heaven will find its own way to deliver your sincere apology for that person you've hurt.

So you don't need to be stuck yourself anymore in the past because all that happened in the past has its own reason you need to unfold. And to do that, you must choose to live in the present and move forward.

Run free without thinking about anything, young one. Let life do its job to let you experience the roller coaster of experiences and lessons as you grow old and learn.

That's how things work.

Attachment Issue

"REMOVE expectations from people, and you'll remove their power to hurt your feelings," - Vex King

Having an attachment issue is a red flag. And that is ok!

Because sometimes, we can't really on-hold ourselves from falling for a being that makes our heart beat differently. We can't really on-hold ourselves from falling for a being that makes our bad days into good days. And for a being that makes our demons slumber.

We can't dictate our hearts for whom to beat because as science says, cardiac muscles are in-voluntary. It is the one who is in control of our blood circulation, and also, for our feelings and emotions.

If it beats to a wrong person, we can't help but to follow it because it is what our heart says and wants. We can't argue about it. We automatically play blind when our heart starts beating fast and loudly to a being we see different, kind, and warm.

So it is ok if you have attachment issues. You are not the one at fault. Your heart is. Blame your heart for feeling different every time someone will try to walk in your life with a different kind of approach. It is not your fault for falling for them. They are warm and kind so I understand. You are innocent.

Nevertheless, honey, it is not ok if you will always let your heart triumph over your mind. It is not ok if you make it a habit to fall for someone who just gives you a slight difference warm like any other and give it a conclusion of many 'maybe's and what if's' in a speed of light the moment you feel special.

Because, young one. Remember this, the moment you conclude something from a soul who just gives you a bare minimum attention that makes your heart jump, that's the start of your agony. Because the moment you expect, the moment you let your heart rule over your sanity.

Expectation is the real antagonist of reality. Expectation is the ugly side of life we can't always disregard because it is good to expect sometimes, to motivate our being to keep it up. To strive for more.

But always remember that in anyways, if you expect too much. To a job, to a thing, or to a person. You will be hurt badly after if your expectation just stayed as an expectation.

It will drain you, exhaust you, and sometimes, it will lead you to get depressed. Especially, if you put a lot of hard work or effort into it and end up not being reciprocated.

So you see, great expectations can lead beings to their own downfall. Especially for a young being like you who can't let his/her heart quite when someone radiant is tickling your peace.

As a matter of factly, attachment issues are the common illnesses of young one's today. Because we are constantly letting our heart rule us when the situation is new and warming.

But to be honest, when it comes to relationships, our mind should rule all of our actions, feelings, emotions, and expectations like a president to a nation so we can minimize the damage to our soul if these being actions are not aligned with his true intention to us.

We save ourselves from expecting too much from a disaster by doing that, and also, we learned by practicing that, the art to not attach easily to things who seem like calm waves in the ocean.

Learn the art of removing your expectations of someone meddling in your life unless he/she stated his true intention to you so you can safeguard your peace and kind heart.

The mind is higher than our heart because it has a reason. Be rational always for new people. Don't expect high from them. Don't let their unverified actions get your knees on the ground and make your mouth drool for them. Always expect less to avoid getting attached.

And if the probability is higher, that you are a kind of being that has a heart that speaks louder than your mind. Then learn the art of 'asking' if someone tries to enter your life.

Ask them what their naked motives are, if you start feeling indifferent from their actions and words. Don't be afraid to ask because it will be your savior from expecting and getting attached to them.

There is no wrong asking them and it is also not embracing. You just want the naked truth from them to protect your inner being. You have all the rights to ask. Always remember that.

Your peace is priceless, young one. Keep note of that. You take months or years building that safe space for yourself so don't let someone destroy it with just a glimpse. Protect your peace by always being rational. Ask what's their real motive and attention first before expecting to avoid self destruction.

Though, if their answer is favored with your expectation. Hug them. Nonetheless, If their answer disappoints you because it is otherwise, learn to breathe it out and ignore them. Don't let them continue what they are doing because action without affirmation is confusing and misleading.

Cut ties with them and go back to that safe place where they first see you happily all by just yourself.

Live again just like before they knock on your door and show them that you are not that soul easily to be taunted by misleading actions because you are fine not accompanied with others.

Walk with grace, young one. Walk.

Relationship Grabber

"**Y**OU must enter a relationship with yourself before anyone else," -Milky and Honey

Being a Relationship Grabber is a red flag. And that is ok!

Because sometimes, we forget to look in our soul first before entering into a commitment that can cause us happiness or heavy baggage. We forget to check kinly ourselves if we are truly ready to settle again after a heart ache and trauma.

We forget to be rational just because someone who is better than our past is now in front of us and giving us the love and affection we wanted to feel for too long. And by that kind of euphoria…

You forget to check if your heart is really empty and ready because of the thrill, warmth, and excitement of the new being in your life showering you.

You forget to consult and question yourself if you are truly ready to commit and give yourself again, 'holistically', to a new soul because you got a slight taste of true love and validation you always crave for that you don't get from your past.

So I really understand you, young one.

It is ok. I really understand. But honey... it is not ok to stay like that. Because you are really being unfair not just to yourself but to that new person as well who has a pure intention of cherishing and keeping you.

Maybe from the start, you enjoy the excitement and warmth that beings give. Maybe from the start, you are thinking that you finally moved on from the past because of overwhelming feelings and satisfaction you are receiving.

But what about that person though? What can you give to that being in exchange if you are still in the midst of questioning yourself if you already moved on? Hence, you let him/her in, in your life without even thinking it deeply because of impulsiveness?

What will happen to that pure soul along the way because of your impulsive decision making? Grabbing his collar and trying to settle in his warm without even considering the pros and cons?

Do you imagine the damage you can create if you make that scenario a reality? Maybe now, no, but may I say, it will be pretty bad and severe for that being.

Because you are more likely, killing that soul by trying to keep him/her, while still picking up your pieces left scattered of your past.

You're trying to keep that being while also trying to find yourself again because you don't want to feel cold and empty handed again during your grieving stage. You don't want to be on that set point again that every minute you are crying and breaking down. That is why you need that being warm to cover up that hollow space in your heart.

And young one, if you are doing that right now to a person. Let that being go. Let him go and give him a chance to love another person because that person doesn't deserve an unstable soul like you.

That person deserves better. And as of the moment, you are not that better because you are in the stage of finding your self worth. You aren't ready to love again. So let go. Give that being a chance to meet a person that has the capability to reciprocate his affection without any hesitation in their system.

Don't be selfish, young one. Don't be too greedy. Learn to let that person go and make him run free so you avoid hurting that pure soul along the way.

Don't give that being trauma your past gives to you—be kind in yourself and for the other souls in the wild.

Don't settle, or don't grab someone's neck if you know you aren't ready to love again. Don't be greedy and selfish. Always take note of this.

You don't need someone to be stable. You don't need someone's shoulder to be better. And specially, you don't need someone to remedy to walk gracefully again into the world.

You only need yourself. Always remember that.

Try to learn the art of self-love, instead of being a relationship grabber. You don't need to get jealous when your friends are already writing their next-best-selling-romance-story while you, still stuck on self love, because you had your perfect time for that. You just need to wait for that great moment to come. Because being into a relationship is both a responsibility and a long commitment.

Prepare yourself to be in that moment while finding your worth in the woods without disturbing any life. Find your soul's craving, alone and with a smile; always remember that you don't need to be in a relationship or justifications of others just to be genuinely happy. No. Never.

You just need companionship, warmth, and validation of yourself to make your being feel alive and full of colors again.

Don't be the start of someone's trauma because you are trying to skip the grieving stage. Because you couldn't do that anyway. It is part of the process we beings, need to always walk on when we fail because that's how realization and lesson put into our souls.

That dark stage is the one who molded our personality to be tough and resilient to every failure for the next challenges the world will serve. Don't be scared at that stage. Hence, learn to hug and love it.

You will realize someday why we, beings, need to always walk in the dark. When you are at that point of your life you see life in a different perspective.

And as you realize it one day, you will just smile at yourself, and ask yourself, "Wow, so that must be it, huh?"

So you see, being a relationship grabber is a red flag. And it is ok! Because we didn't know it. But as you come this far, there is no reason for you to be like a relationship grabber.

Remember this young one, being in a hoe stage is not cool. It is gross because you let other souls suffer and hope for you even though you can't really commit to their beings.

Wake up, young one. Learn how to be better and kind to others. It is not cool to be the cause of trauma and a person's heart ache.

Dictator

"THE ego wants quantity but the soul want quality" - Quotes 'nd Notes

Being a dictator in a relationship or in anything is a red flag. And that is ok!

Because... do we really know to ourselves that we are being dictator to a thing or to another being's life?

Do we ask this before ourselves if our decisions and wants are beneficial for both souls? Do we also try even once to step back for a second to check our whole being if we are really being like that?

No. Not even once. We never even think of doing that. Because we always see our decisions as righteous. We see ourselves as always right. We see ourselves as perfect and rational beings all the time. That we forget that in reality, we are just humans.

Beings who have just evolved over the centuries that also had flaws and imperfections. And sometimes, our decisions and wants are just too over-lapsing for the sanity of other beings.

We literally step by step, caging their humanity in our hands because of our heavy demands and wants to them. We do that because we see in our own perspective that it is just the right thing to do—but is it really?

Is it really the best and right thing for them, or do you just want to be the dominant one? You just want to control and manipulate that person to your own wants and will for your own satisfaction so you are acting like a King in that being life?

Do you truly love that soul? Or you just want something to control? Ask yourself thrice and think again thrice for your answer and leave what doesn't and resonate what you reflected.

Because young one, the things that you are doing, being a dictator to someone's life, is just way too exhausting. Mentally and physically. It is also draining their emotions towards you because what you are giving to them is not love—it is oppression.

And young one, I'm telling you. If you will not let go of that habit, being a dictator, all your cherished and for-keep souls will walk away from you because they can't stand your overwhelming self-righteousness. You will just drain the beings who will try to love and care you if you keep being like that. You will always put their love to a boiling test tube and make their soul chained because they can't do anything instead you let them be. And it is not love, honey—it is torturing.

You are not always right, always remember that. And to a relationship or in anything, you shouldn't decide alone what will do because the decision you will make will affect other lives.

Learn the art of letting your partner go. Do not cage them in your warmth because if you do, they will not grow as a beautiful person. Also, you. You will not grow because you are only focusing on someone else's life rather than your own growth and development.

Learn the art of loving another being without killing their personal dreams, wants, and desires because that is already engraved in their system before they know you. Let them achieve things and learn to clap your hands in the audience if they do. Do not be their antagonist to not make it to the summit. Rather, be your partner's loyal side-kick who was always there for their ups and downs.

Don't be so full of yourself, young one. Be brave to seek help from your partner because that is naturally the thing you will do if you can't decide. Do not make impulsive decisions if you know the situation is hot. You are not alone in the relationship. Always use healthy communication to make better decisions for both of you.

Make it a habit to ask your being what is the best decision for both of you. Make it a habit to not decide alone. Make it a habit to not always see yourself as a righteous person. Because honey, that is a red flag. A big one. Nonetheless, it is ok.

You can still change though, because the life of a human is a never ending work-in-progress. You get enlightened, you learn, you adopt the lesson.

We must accept the mere fact that we are not always right, young one. Keep that. Sometimes, we are the ones who are making mistakes. We can't just admit it in all our bones because we picture ourselves as perfect beings already.

We think highly of ourselves that we forget that we are work-in-progress beings who are vulnerable to making huge mistakes sometimes.

We fucked up. And that is ok! It is normal. What is not, is you do not swallow it and learn from it. What is not is, you don't accept it because you are always in the denial stage. That you think you are always right, that leads you to being a dictator.

Evolved, honey. Evolved. Don't stay in that phase for too long. It is intoxicating. You will just hurt your soon loved ones if you stay like that. You will drain and exhaust them if you keep being a self-centered soul who doesn't embody and reflect his own mistakes.

Grow up. Mistakes and failures are not one of the ugly sides of the world to hate. Hence, it is one of the fundamental ingredients for us beings to be more beautiful and gracious people.

Learn to hug your mistakes. Learn to love it. Because soon, you realize that mistakes will follow you for the rest of your life because you are a forever work-in-progress being just like others. You will also soonly see how life really works. And you will understand the beauty process of life.

Ego wants quantity, as the quotes saids. It is where our dictator self lives. Nonetheless, the soul want quality. And our soul is where we live. The us that has flaws and imperfections. You just gonna choose between the two who will rule your soul everyday.

But remember, beings and souls who have imperfect attributes in them are what is loved the most out of many. Especially, when you are all loud and proud to say it. To say that you are a, "Work-in-progress and spirits of life and wonders are working in me."

Because who wouldn't fall for that anyway? Braveness. Naked truths—we can't ask for more. And on the other side, we can't fall in-love and get smitten by a Ken-Like-In-The-Barbie-Series, right? No. Never. This is the reality we are talking about. And here, there is no really Ken.

Maybe there is, but are we really sure that that's the real them? No. Because too perfect characters are misleading. So don't be one. Don't be a Ken or Barbie.

Be you young one, be you. Because the world is now full of lies and fakes. What we only need right now is a person who is love language is telling the truth. Keep note of that.

Impulsive Decision Maker

"**Y**OU can't make decisions based on fear and possibility of what might happen" -Michelle Obama

Being an Impulsive decision maker is a real red flag. And that is ok!

You see, I understand why you are like that.

I understand why you are always scared and fritten to the possibility of what might happen next — you are just scared of your own actions outcomes, that is why you are trying to make a decision on your own without thoroughly thinking.

I really understand, honey. You don't need to feel suffocated or feel attacked right now. I've been in that quiet and dark place. So I really understand you. I am not here to judge you. I am here to give your soul warm embraces because that is what you really need.

Because sometimes, we are overly thinking about things to the future because we are traumatized in our past heart aches. We don't want it to happen to us next time, that is why our senses are more alert right now.

We don't want to be in that dark phase again in our life, that is why our defenses are on their high level. And one small action from a being that gives chill similarities to our late trauma's—we will make conviction without thinking of them. We will cut them off from our life to safeguard our hearts and peace because we know that pattern will just give us anxiety.

You've been there. You know the feeling. You the agony. You know how it will end up. That is why you are more alert than ever. That is why you make it a habit to overthink things that might happen so you can avoid the damage if you see the similar patterns you've been through.

I know how you feel, honey. I know. I validate it. But—you must know too that being like that is a red flag.

Because you see, before, I thought it was good to be like that.

To be like a walking-time-bomb in a relationship, where every move of my partner is must according to what I just know, because if it doesn't, I will explode automatically. I will overthink things and I will start making and concluding things. And at the end—I will make a decision alone for us, that soon, will torment and hunt me because of injustices.

I thought before that it is ok to be like that. To make it a habit because I believed before, some day, someone who has a great intention to take care of my soul will knock at my door and give me the love and assurance my mind deserves. Before, my way of thinking was relying on other beings to find me and hold me in my lowest. Before, I was a fan of waiting for my special someone who would fix and love me for who I am. Because before—I always believed in that 'perfect timing' and 'perfect person'. I am one of those folklore fanatics.

That was me before, honey. So I know where you are coming from.

But as I get older, and when I step into adulthood. I realized, that the person I am waiting to mend me is really taking his time on the road walking and wandering.

Or maybe, that person I am waiting for is still another being warm, taking what lesson he will take to that person. Or maybe, that person I am constantly waiting for is just focusing on his own character-development, that is why he is taking too long to come at me and love. Maybe... so many maybes and what if's I realized.

But the important thing I resonate in myself while on my darkest days is—independence, acceptance and self-worth.

Independence because I just realize that I can't put the burden I carried to another soul because it is torturing. It is not their job to fix my instability. To heal me. To cure me. I realized that my healing and development is my own responsibility and job for myself.

Acceptance. I accepted that my meant-to-be-being can't take my emergency call right now because he is busy finding his own too. He is busy finding himself and busy trying to love someone as of the moment he thinks is the one for him. I accept that fact and try to stand on my own feet while my knees are trembling. I stand and start investing more goodness in my mind so I can find my own refuge and solace within me. To keep my demon quiet and caged.

And self-worth. My self worth. I realized I must raise my own appraisal for my own good to feel high and graceful for myself again. So I can stand everyday and make a change in myself step by step so I can be the best of me even in the small steps I make.

So you see, being a red flag is ok because it is the phase of human being we can't escape. Because here, in real life, there are no such perfect beings. There is no such person existing without even a single flaw and imperfection in their bones. We all have one, always remember that. You are not alone.

Maybe, the one you see who you think has the greenest character is the product of life. A product of the red flag phase. And a product of self-growth, self-realization, and change. They are like that because they have the courage to change themselves—and so do you.

Learn to have the courage in your soul to change for yourself. To appraise your self-worth not for others validation and acceptance but for your own good. Learn the art of not expecting for someone to fix you. Acquired your own independence in yourself. Own yourself as you should. Mark your whole being and soul as your real estate and no one can hurt any part of it without your permission.

Learn to let go of that toxic stereotype that we, beings, need to accompany to be better. No. Never. Maybe somehow, true. But in the whole process? No. You only need yourself. So try to fix what you need to fix yourself.

Heal yourself, young one. Pick up the broken pieces of your trust by yourself and stay just like you are. Kind, loving, and passionate. Don't lose fate for life. He just gives you the wrong person to know who you will let in next time and who will be just ignored.

Fix your trust issue with yourself. Always believe that life has many things to offer as you grow and learn in his care. Maybe now, you are breaking because the being he gives you, traumatizes you. Maybe now, you are in your lowest point and self questioning because of what happened. But honey, whatever life serves you. Don't lose faith in humanity. Don't lose your faith that someday, the world will be kind to you and you will meet the right and perfection to you.

But for now—try to stand up and fix yourself first. Ready yourself for that person so you can both be happy and ready when you finally meet each other gazes in the middle of the road or bump into each other in the coffee shop in the morning hour. Fix your trust issue and unstable mind for yourself and for the greatest love you are waiting for.

So when the time has come, that you feel, you finally meet that person you've been waiting for—you are ready. Emotionally. Mentally. And Physically. You are ready to give him your genuine embrace without self distracting because you are whole inside you and no one can break you aside yourself.

Overload Expectation

"ALWAYS hope, but never expect. Always believe, but don't expect for a return"

Having overload expectations is a red flag. And that is ok!

Because the truth is, sometimes, we expect because actions with meanings are serves in us. We expect because someone is giving us that different chill that makes our bones dripping and alive. We expect because we see hope and light in their actions. And it is ok.

It is not your fault to feel indifferent. It is not your fault that you expect based on their actions. It is not your fault to fall for them and hope for their being.

But honey, it is not ok to stay like that. To have always overload expectations to things or to a person.

You will only hurt yourself on the road if you keep hoping for great possibilities and outcomes because of just their actions. Always remember—action without conviction is misleading. Think smart, work smart. Don't let your heart beat be the cause of your false hopes and downfall. Restrain your heart from beating to a unknown intention of a new being in your life.

Before you expect from someone, you must feel their eagerness to hold you badly by their words and actions. Don't let their words confuse you. Don't let their mere action mislead you to your own heartbreak.

Don't eat if they just serve you with just their words or sugar coated promises. No. It must be both always if they want you. Words with conviction and action with clear and great intention.

Because if they serve you with just flowery words and misleading actions, they don't want you. They do not like you. They don't want you enough to level up—what they only want is for you to get confused.

Stay away from beings who just give you a bare minimum affection. No honey. Don't eat leftovers. You don't deserve it. You have been through a lot to be just where you are right now.

Don't let those who just want validation for themselves harm your peace. Cut them off if their actions are not aligned with their true intention.

Learn the art of not giving a damn to things who speak uncertainties. Learn the art of not allowing people to destroy your peace and break your growth by just their different fire and scent.

Don't always expect high from beings who is love language is killing their partner with anxiety because their actions are more powerful than their true intention to them.

Don't settle for a being that only gives you butterflies in your stomach but not peace in your mind. You are worth more than that.

You deserve better so cut that soul off from your life and start being alone again. Embrace your being on the process alone without the accompaniment of any souls. You can do it. You can surpass it. You can survive it. Don't let the darkness and loneliness taunt you to find someone. Hug yourself.

Someday, Apollo will pull the sun again in your life. Just be brave. Just have faith in the process. Have always the courage to walk out in a room or to a person's life who only gives you bare minimum energy and only exhausts you.

Build your walls and boundaries so you will never be a fool again by your own overloading expectations. Learn to recognize the patterns as you grew from those humans who give you trauma and hard times. So you know what human you will let into your door.

Always remember, don't put a lot of expectations on someone or on something. Stay ignorant to their actions until they confess their true intention to you. Don't give a damn about them unless they stated they want you badly and they shower you with assurance and firm actions.

Don't let your wild imagination rule you if someday, a being will come to your life and give you a different feeling and affection you haven't felt before.

No honey, that is a trap from falling. Always put your expectations to the lowest. Always tell yourself that beings who will come to your life have different purposes so you can avoid breaking your own soul.

Clear your mind always when someone is trying to enter your heart. Don't hug their warmth fast. Don't look up to their face and hope for possibility about both of you, turning to a 'us'.

Learn the art of calming down your horses and let just the spirits guide your mind and soul along the way.

You don't need other beings to feel great satisfaction. You don't need others to be your refuge and solace. You have yourself already. And that is enough. Don't expect. Stay away from expectation because overloaded expectations are the red flag we must try to diminish in us.

Because the truth is, sometimes, overloaded expectations kill a dreamer and a wanderer. Always remember that. So be careful. Protect your soft spot at all times and stop your expectations for any beings. Rather, focus on your own growth and development.

Untamed Jealousy

"JEALOUSY is just lack of self-confidence"

Having an untamed jealousy in your system is a red flag. And that is ok!

Jealousy is everyone's enemy. It is not only you. It is everyone. We get jealous because we see something in someone that we don't have. We see in them our greatest insecurities that we wish for centuries for all the sentinels in the world to be in us, but they don't.

You see, everyone gets jealous. But Honey— too jealousy will kill you. Stop that. It is a red flag.

Too jealousy or untamed jealousy will make your radiant lose its light. You will get scared everyday, every minute, every hour to show yourself to the world or to your someone because you have a perfect figure living in yourself that you badly want to imitate. But in truth, all those double standards you set for yourself are just too surreal. It is impossible.

No one is a perfect young one, always remember that. Stop choking yourself by your own insecurities. We beings are born to be imperfect and we must accept that fact. We can never be perfect. We can never be too great.

But—why do we, beings, always obsessed about perfection by the way?

Do you ask yourself that question already why your insecurities are born in you? Why are you fretting about showing your scars and wounds to anybody?—Why are you hiding your true self from anyone?

Because the truth is, why we want to be perfect, we want to be that light that everyone will look up to. That person who voices a flawless personality; we want validation for others that is why we are always so hyped to be flawless. And that fact, you must resonate in yourself.

Indenial is just a monkish act. Said by a great philosopher. So don't deny it. Take that and get hurt badly. You deserve it.

Wake up, young one. You are being blinded to others' light rather than your own light. You want to be like those flawless beings you see that you are starting to change yourself just to be fit for what you believe is 'true beauty'. But the truth is, there is no 'true beauty'. Only diverse beauty from all the billions of beings is what we have.

Diverse beauty of beings are what make this planet colorful and wonderful. Difference of each soul is what makes us beautiful. Always remember that.

You don't need to follow the double standard of the society. Be your own. Be different. Be unknown. You are you for a reason, and they are they for a reason too.

You don't get to be jealous of anyone; physically, mentally, academically, and financially. You are born and built that way because it has a reason. You just need to believe in yourself first to unfold what is that reason.

Be brave. You don't need validation or admiration of everyone. You just need your own acceptance and that's good. You are ready to go forward to grow and develop.

Take care of yourself. Mentally and physically. Don't drool over anyone's validation. Invest in what you put in your mind and always be kind to everyone. These are just the formulas you need to make your light more stunning. You don't need anything else more than that.

You don't need to change yourself. You just need to improve and be more developed.

Learn the art of not looking to any double standards. You will just suffocate yourself if you will. Just grow and learn. That is all you need.

Someday, when the stars align perfectly, beings who are astonished to your soul will come and embrace your difference. They will accept you for who you are and they will not tell you to change any bits of you because you are perfect as you are right now.

Someday, someone with great intention of loving you will come and hug those insecurities and differences of yours like hugging to the stem of a rose. That being will be whipped by your uniqueness and will always tell you that you are beautiful and perfectly fine everyday and every moment you are together. That being will proudly hold your hand in the crowd without any bit of hesitation while smiling at you widely with those sparkling eyes of his.

Someday, someone who has the courage to love you will come. And you, who win in the trial with double standards of the society versus yourself will be willingly to let that being enter your life because you have no anything to lose.

You survived to choose yourself everyday and build your own standard for yourself. It is just right, when the time has come that the stares of the people to you will not bother you, to fall in love and be happy.

Falling in love without jealousy in your system is like being in euphoria because you will not be insecure and fret to anyone who will come close to your palangga because you know to yourself that only your different radiant can attract and make his head turned 360.

You see, without too much jealousy. You have your peace. Without too much insecurities. You have no fear of losing things or to a person.

So wake up young one, let go of that red flag already and fly for development. People who have an unstable system like you can't hold someone's hand firmly and tightly if every minute, you are being insecure and jealous. You will just kill that pure soul's love for you, and at the end, based on true tendencies, that person will leave you because of exhaustion or a bad understanding of you.

So go young one, evolve. Make a change to yourself. Walk in the light and release that bad habit. Try the formula I give you and try to love yourself first before anyone else.

Give a break in any relationship. You don't need it as of the moment. It will naturally knock at your door once life feels you are ready for that. So for now, focus on your evolution as a being.

Focus on yourself. Love yourself every day and every moment. Make your souls feel that she is loved and cherished. So no light of someone she can recognize except in yours.

Run wild young one, bloom.

Insensitive

"MANNERS are a sensitive awareness of the feelings of others. If you have that awareness, you have good manners, no matter which fork you use" -Emily Post

Being an insensitive person is a red flag. And that is ok!

Because sometimes, you don't really know what to do with a new plot served at your face. You are new to the things that's why you are not familiar with the traits and patterns of how they really work.

So yes. It is ok young one. It is ok. Breathe.

But always remember, it is not ok to stay like that. To stay being an insensitive person to anything or to a relationship because you will just give heart arches to the pure souls who will try to risk for you if you stay like that.

You will only stab their heart by your ignorance. You will choke them. You will leave them breathless.

So honey, please. Change. Have the courage to let go of that heavy baggage and try to be a better being.

Don't be too insensitive to beings who only try to love you. Don't be a hard person to them. Reciprocate their feelings and try to learn the art of falling in love. Risk if they will risk their whole life for you. Fall if you genuinely want to. Don't be insensitive to others feelings. It is traumatizing.

Don't give them bare minimum attention and feelings. That is being insensitive already. Give them the love that they deserve. Give them the love that they wanted for you and for once, learn to be happy.

In a relationship, both hearts are at stake. If you are an insensitive person, then you don't deserve to enter a relationship because you will just invalidate someone's feelings without knowing it. You will just be someone's greatest trauma she will always pray every night never wanting to feel again.

You are just like caging your partner into a bird prison. You make them feel like that becauase in any situation, you are acting like a fucking ignorant.

You are acting like you don't know what to do, but in reality, you do. You know what to do. Your heart knows what to do in that situation. It is shouting at you. You know how to fix the misunderstanding, the misconception, and the problem but you choose to ignore it. To act like a blind man the whole damn time. And your partner—you always leave that being hung in the mid air together with your problems and try to just forget it without even talking about it.

Confess it, confess now and tell yourself you are like that. That you are that person who always chooses to flight in a fight-or-flight situation because you don't know what to do and how to handle things. Confess it that you are that person who always invalidates someone's feelings in the most insensitive way. Confess it now young one, self denial is inevitable. You will just stay ignorant for the rest of your life if you do.

Accept the fact that you are a walking red flag and no one will love and embrace you if you stay like that. Accept the fact that you need to let go of that heavy baggage and need to say deeply sorry for those souls you have broken and hearts shattered from your past.

Say sorry to those people you hurt badly. They deserve it. Reminisce all bullshit you do while you are their aray of light. Reminisce all the problems you ignored. Reminisce all the scenes when that poor soul from your past is trying to ask you for assurance but in return, you just give them confusing actions.

Reminisce young one, reminisce. Remember all the pain and heart aches you caused and reflect.

Learn from all of those and change. Because honey, it is hard to stay like that forever. No one can love you that way. Every being has a limitation. Don't always expect that someday, someone who has great intention of understanding that bad habit of yours will come and kiss you deeply. No. There is no such thing like that.

Every soul gets tired. Every soul who tries to love you will get tired if you stay like that. No, honey. No one will stay. Beings will always leave you crying.

So change, young one. Resonate your lesson and leave that habit behind. You can be more beautiful than right now. Don't be afraid if someday, someone will use your past against you. Don't be disheartened if someday, someone will not believe you are already a changed human just because they know you from your old version. Hence, keep going. Keep being a better person.

Ready yourself rather for that someone who will enter your life again. Improve your soul. So whenever the day has come and that being, smile and say hi to you. You can smile back and say hello without any anxiety that you might hurt that being just like your past because you are now a changed person. A more beautiful version of yourself.

You see, imagining being a better person can get your blood regulation normal. It keeps your heart beating fast because you are getting excited to see that better version of yourself if you will just try and start your development now.

Always remember honey, being a red flag is ok because it is a phase we beings need to walk on because that is where our greatest mistakes were made. There is where our big bang realization began. And there is where we always find the courage to evolve—to grow.

So honey, it is ok. Let me hug you. You don't need to feel embarrassed because of your mistakes. You are just a being. And it is already a part of us, falling down, as long as we keep breathing. It is part of the life process. Don't feel embarrassed. Embrace it. That is your symbol of survival and your victory to move forward to the light.

Added; always remember too, that, being a walking red flag for the rest of your life is not ok. You need to let that go and be better.

Keep note of that.

Too Much Asking For Validation

"YOUR self worth does not belong in the hands of other people"-
Ashley Hetherington

Too much asking for validation is a red flag. And that is ok.

You just don't know your place, that is why you are begging for people to give your pure heart and soul the validation you wanted and you think you really deserve—it is ok.

It is ok if you are in that given situation right now where you are begging to a being to validate you. To validate your existence in their life. To make yourself fit into their room everyday by showering them your whole you. It is ok, young one. It is ok. We all have been there.

But honey, just like I thought you. It is not ok to stay like that. To stay like a beggar for their attention and affection. To stay imprisoned to people or to someone who doesn't see your worth. To stay like a ready-to-go substitute when the original cannot go. No honey. You don't deserve to be treated that way. They don't deserve a pure soul like you. Walk away in that place already. It is killing you inside. I know. So let go.

Walk away in someone's or to people's life if they make you feel you are not enough and your presence is not required. Walk away if they make you feel not-special. Walk away if you want to tell a story to them but they choose to set aside that topic and hear the next one rather. No honey. Your soul doesn't deserve to be treated that way. Don't force yourself in a room that doesn't feel like your home. No.

Walk out if they make you feel you are not welcome even if it will definitely break you into dust. Don't stay.

Walk away for your peace. For yourself. Save yourself. Don't mind the damage and the loss. You can make yourself beautiful alone. You don't need a person or people like that.

Don't dedicate yourself or your whole being to the wrong people or person. No. It is a big red flag that you must not make a habit or a living.

Don't ask for validation from any beings. Don't ask them to pity you. Don't ask them to look into your eyes the same as you look at them with compassion and pure love. No. Never ask for validation.

Don't ask them to feel the same way you feel for them. Don't ask for sympathy or importance. No honey. Never do that.

You don't need to ask someone or anyone for your soul's cravings. Because you know—the right person or people will not let you do it.

The right person or people will naturally do what makes your demons calm and sleep. Always remember that. You don't need to ask for anyone's validation and attention because the right one will always look you in the eyes and will tell you that you are a blessing from heaven that God's given to be their lamp in the dark.

You are more than enough. You are enough already to be valid. Always take note of that.

So if by any chances, that as of the moment you are begging for someone or people to validate your existence—stop.

Get your senses back. Wipe your tears and stand up. Then, with grace together with your peace, walk out. Walk away from their lives and start finding your real haven.

That person doesn't deserve you, honey. Promise. I cross my heart.

You deserve more than that. You deserve a better person or companion. Don't kneel and beg for those beings attention. Those beings don't deserve you! Know your worth! Know your heart and peace price! Know you are enough and you deserve more than that!

Learn the art of not begging for anyone's validation. You can master it as long as you have faith in yourself. You don't need anyone to achieve it either. You can do it alone.

Just don't mind being alone in the process honey. Hug the peace the quiet road gives you as you walk by and realize that you are a wonderful person and you are enough.

Learn the art of being your own 911 in case you want to feel valid. Valid yourself. Valid your whole being.

Fall in love with yourself and strengthen your inner core so you will not beg for any soul in the future the validation you wanted because you already acquired it all by yourself.

Be proud and make that as your standpoint to shout to yourself that 'you are enough' and 'you don't deserve bare minimum love'. You are sick to eat those. Learn to change the course of food set in you. Learn to decline and learn to ask for better because you deserve to be served right.

So you see, too much asking for validation is a red flag. But remember—it is ok. We can't miss walking along that terrible road because there, we find our courage to change. To be wise.

There, we find the true essence of our self worth and how to protect it. And finally—we know in that dark place that our self worth does not belong to other people. It is ours. It is always and always will be on you. Always remember that.

So walk young one. Change. Bear the cold wind and the loneliness. You can do it. It is better to be stuck in that place. Do that for yourself and not others. Your soul needs you.

One Sided POV

" "YOU will make mistakes. That is inevitable. Learn to swallow that fact as you grow"

Having one sided point of view all the time is a red flag. And that is ok.

Because sometimes, we can't just admit to ourselves that in often situations, we are the cause of trouble. We can't admit to our soul that sometimes, our decisions are not right and our plan is not really for the betterment of everyone. Because what our mind thinks is we are always right. We think, our way of thinking is way better than anyone else's; that is our natural disease as humans as we grow and learn in the way.

We think to ourselves that we are already unfolding the secrets of the world—we think we are more superior to any individual in the room just because of our victories and milestones possessed.

But no honey, let me tell you something—you are wrong. It is not just the experiences or how traumatizing your life in the past is the basis all the time. You are wrong. We beings have different kinds of paths. Always remember that.

Don't base your conclusion and conviction on your own experiences because if you do

—you might probably let someone fall. You will probably miss making a better decision, action, or advice to another soul who is lost because what you give to that soul is just a pang of your peace you wanted to brag out and not the advice that person truly needed.

No honey. Don't do that. Don't be self reliant. Don't depend on your own thinking and perspective. That is a red flag.

You make your people that surround you suffocate because you only see the goodness and the truth in your own light. You are always on the one side. On your side. You only see everything in yourself and not what others really condition. Don't deny it. I know. The people arounds you know. They just can't tell you because they are afraid of what your reaction will be.

You know it too. You have the feeling. Your soul speaks at you. Your conscience tickles you. You just don't want to admit it. You just don't want to change because alas, you think you are right. You think you are in the right standpoint and the beings in your environment are wrong.

And honey, let me tell you this—that is a bad habit.

Learn to let it go. Learn to crave for more wisdom and knowledge life will offer you. Don't be satisfied with yourself now. Open your doors widely and always for new construction and changes in you.

Don't be so self righteous and self centered. It will make you a lonely being. Hence, learn the art of staying ignorant.

Ignorant in a way that you will not think you are already perfectly made and that is enough already. No young one. No. Always stay on the process and don't make your soul be content in your version right now just because you think you are already good at.

No honey, that is bad. Don't get tired of evolving as a better person. Learn to love it and take it as your guideline to more greatness, the Supreme being in the heaven plan for you.

Continue to seek for improvement. Ask your someone or friends their opinion about you and try to digest without any heavy feeling their criticism.

Accept the fact that you are not perfect and you will never be. It is ok. No one is. Either me, or everyone. No one.

We beings are always stuck in the process of life. And as soon as you divert your eyes to the other side, you will understand someday that being stuck as a working-progress-person is what makes us human. What makes us beautiful beings. Because that endless road that our souls are walking is what mold us to our greatest version.

Be a more open minded young one. Don't always stick your eyes in your shadow. In your light. In yourself. Look around and resonate that the world is not always round to you. Life is not favored to you either—so be socially conscious. Leave that bad habit of yours, being self sided and righteous.

No one will love a being like you because your eyes only linger on yourself if you stay like that. So please honey, grow. It is not too late to get back into being a work in progress.

You may be stuck for too long, but honey. Always remember that as long as your nasal breath out a warm air from your lungs, you can grow. You can dream. You can be better.

The world has many things to offer. Don't give up. Don't be stuck in that place. Run again. Leap again. Walk again. The sun is waiting for you to come out in that dark cave honey. Move. You can do it.

Leave that phase and be a great person. So when one day, in any circumstances, your greatest someone will appear in front of you. You can face that being eye to eye without any hesitation in your system because of that time. You are already a changed person.

You not only look in your own light but rather in everyone's different radiant and vibrant. You learned already that you will not be a great being, and always will not be because someone will always be better in you and clockwise. You learned already by that time that as long as you are breathing and keep going, your soul will always be stuck in the process. And also, by that time, you learned to accept the fact that you are just human and you are always vulnerable to fall. To make mistakes.

You see, if you start now to change yourself, you can attain more self validation from the world. You can spread your wings more widely and can go as far and high as you want if you just don't cage yourself to your comfort zone.

Be more courageous to explore honey. The world is beautiful even though it is not perfect. Explore every bit of it and try to understand how beautiful human life can be.

You can do it, young one. Your better version is rooting for you.

Silent Treatment Issue

"**S**ILENT treatment is for third graders and people who can't sort out their problem"

If you have the mannerism to stay silent all the times when something isn't right and keep it all up until it becomes heavy, you are a red flag. But—that is ok. You can still move that bad habit aside. It is not too late to remove it.

You see, if you are in a relationship right now and your soul always goes silent whenever you both, your partner, is having a hard time. You just make that person lose it light to you.

If you keep acting like a mad-mute-person whenever you feel something that triggers your anxiety or past, you just make people around you tired. Mentally.

You make them uncious by that silent treatment habit of yours. You make them think endlessly of what happened to you and why you just walk away. You will make beings around you ask themselves, what is their problem and what is wrong with them and why you just left them breathless and hanging. Why do you suddenly fly off to a place they can't touch you. Why did you just leave them?

You see, that bad habit kills a pure soul untainted sanity. Remove that within you because if you keep that toxic mannerism, everyone's get tired of you. Everyone who will try to love you will be traumatized and will undergo the questioning process on their debts, what is really the problem? They or… you?

You. You are the problem honey. That silent treatment of yours is the big problem we have. Accept it. There is no other way to overcome that phase if you will not just admit to yourself that you are a fucking red flag that brings heart aches and a can of tears in someone's life. Accept it and reconcile your mistakes.

Accept that it is wrong to not address the problem when you have all the chances to speak about it. Accept that, being silent in a situation or expressing your feelings to someone who wants to win your heart is a red flag and a very confusing act because instead of trying to open your vulnerable side to that person, you just hide your inner self even more because you are scared of the possibilities of showing to someone your vulnerable delicate side.

But young one, in that situation and perfect timing—just be you. Don't be afraid to show your naked imperfect soul to someone who is trying to enter into your life to let them familiarize your wounds and scars from the past trauma's you survive and overcome.

Show them the ugly picture of your personality and test their perseverance and love for you in that situation. Check if after you show them your naked soul they will still and embrace you. Check if after they see your ugly and weak other half, they still love you abundantly.

Because young one, if they do. Don't let that being escape in your fingertips. Grab that someone's collar and kiss that person instantly because finally, you meet the other half of you who can see you beautiful and graceful despite your flaws and imperfections. Do it honey, do it. Love that person and try to give him/her the chance to make you feel precious and important.

They are the right one. So please. Don't give them trauma. Try step by step; learn the art of having the courage to tell that person what you are truly feeling and think whenever both of you are having a misunderstanding.

Don't let your worries and what if's overcome you. Don't let your negative thoughts dictate your decision. Be a better human. Learn to ask if you have to. Tell the naked truth if you want. Spoke what your heart says. Be transparent to yourself and to your someone. Be fair.

Don't let the day come that, the person who sees you as their sunshine sees you as their catastrophe. Don't let their love fall out just because everytime you fight, quarrel, or argue you just give it a silent feedback.

No honey. Don't let that day come because I am telling you—if that day comes and that someone asks to leave your side because of your own fault for having a low courage to speak your heart out loud to them, promise—it will break your heart to shreds.

You will cry all night in your room while your heart is heaved beating. You will blame yourself everyday because of your cold actions towards that person. You will reminisce about all your mistakes from the past and no matter how you wanted to go back to those times so you can fix everything you do to that person, you can't. You can't go back because that's already the past.

I've been there. I know the creepy and depressing feeling in that phase so I don't want you to experience that. So please, young one— change yourself. Be moved.

Remove the word silent treatment in your system. Practice having the courage day by day to express yourself to people who are in your life.

Don't think about their judgment of you because right people who want to really know every bit of your bones will never get tired of unveiling every bit of it. Remember that. Remember, right human beings will be interested while the wrong people will only just stare.

Mix Signals Aren't Healthy

"INDECISION is still a decision. If you like someone. Say it. Don't give that person mix signals and mental chaos"

For the last time, giving mixed signals to a soul that sees you as their heroine is a red flag. But, for the last time too. It is ok!

Because sometimes, you can't just know how to say your feelings to everyone. You can't just tell them how you really feel. And sometimes, accept it or not, it is just so good to be just there. To be in the middle of everything — in chaos. Receiving anything you wanted for granted.

But honey, let me tell you this for the last time too. It is not ok to stay like that. To always be on the winning side.

To be always the one who always receives love, passion, care, dedication, and heart sweats. Because honey, if you just stay there for the rest of your life without committing to any beings who give those to you, at the end of the day, it is your loss. I say it again. It is your loss.

Because you see, being in the middle of anything isn't always healthy. Sometimes, you are being so much. I understand too that—you are overwhelmed by the warmth and kisses that person gives you. But—how about that person anyway? Do you check that soul status? Is that person's heart is ok in your set up?

You being in the middle, while that person is on your side? Waiting for you to move?

Do you picture yourself already after what I've said? Do you already picture how ugly you are right now? Or still not?

Do you just realize now that you are being an unfair human being to that person who is trying to move your heart? Because honey—yes. You are being unfair. A fucking unfair.

Because you see, you are just in the middle without knowing anything at all in everyone's life. You are there getting all the attention and care you wanted. But what about them? What about those people in their standpoint? They are exhausted. They are tired already for always trying to move you in your thrown but didn't an inch you move because you are fucking enjoying all the satisfaction.

You are being unfair in a way that you are enjoying. While those beings are deadly confused and anxious about what's the score between the two of you.

You are being unfair in a way that you are in euphoria because of the affection you are getting while that person is in agony because you want them to stay but don't want to commit for their sanity.

You are being unfair in a way that, you like to hold their hand and want them to stay because they are warm but can't even think to touch their heart and reciprocate their feelings just because you can't see their images in your future. But still, you want to cherish the moment because you are receiving all the satisfaction and attention you wanted.

You see, you are a red flag. A really freaking one. Wake up human. Mind others feelings and not just yours all the damn time. If you don't like the being who is trying their very best to win you. Tell them. Shout to them. Push them away!

Don't hold their hand or just give them a little hope to stay because they will just get confused and will hope really hard for both of you. If you don't like the being, kindly give them a warm hug and explain why you can't risk their souls. Why can't you give back the love and attention they invested in you.

Be kind in a way you will say out your feelings to a person that doesn't move the butterflies in your stomach. Reject them in a way they can digest. It is better to give them false hope and at the end, when things are really getting deep and alarming, you will cut that beings wings and just leave like nothing happened.

Stop being unfair, young one. Stop being like you right now. You don't know how it feels to be just left hanging. To be just so broken because you really hope for something but at the end it is all nothing.

To be just an easy-go-lucky and generous being who risks everything in their heart but at the end, they will lose everything including themselves; You don't know how it feels to be a fallen grace. So please, be kind. Be kind to those pure beings.

Don't move them if you don't mean to. Don't ask them to stay if you can't commit. And lastly, don't give them mixed signals to get what you want. It is selfishness. It is the red flag beings have ever had. Mix signals.

Because you see—souls like you are the reason why there are overthinker people. Why are people scared of their past. Why do people have attachment issues. Why people are relationship grabbers. Why are there people who are dictators. Why people are impulsive decision makers. Why people have overloaded expectations, untamed jealousy, insensitivity, and so on. Named it. I will blame all those to beings like you because you are the trauma's everyone wishes they will never have.

You are a big walking red flag. Accept it, young one. Accept it. You are the cause of so many heart breaks and breakdowns. You are the reason why someone is crying silently in their own room right now. You are the reason why they are in a dark place, losing. Why does someone not believe in love anymore. You are the cause of all of that. Always remember that.

Nevertheless, thanks to people like you, humans change. Thanks to your red flag; someone already knows her worth. Her soul. Herself. Thanks to your red flag—someone is in the process right now of becoming a great and strong individual the world can't wait to see.

You see, it is ok to be like that. Your red flag is the tool why someone is winning life right now. Why is someone now at his/her best life right now. And why is someone now trying to change. You are the cause of all of that. So I thank you.

But honey, how about you? Do you really wanna stay just like that? You are being left behind. Move. Wake up. Evolved. Start removing that bad habit of yours. Start moving forward and leave that toxic phase.

Have the courage to leave in that middle standpoint and walk to the path life prepared just for you. Unveil things that make your heart excited. Go to places that make your eyes linger in any place. Go where your heart beats. Find your own home. Find your own refuge and solace. It is your time now to change. To go home where you belong.

Find yourself. Fall in love with the process and look if things excites you and make your bones dripping. Don't settle if you are not ready. Build up your career first. Fulfill all your dreams and reach the summit first if you want. Go. Fly high. Dream high.

Fall in love with yourself and resonate with your past. Reflect on those and be a better human and a lover. Because honey, in this world full chaos. What we only need right now is a being who has the courage to always move forward and try to change for the betterment.

So go, honey! Love life can wait. Settle if you are truly ready. Change first. Be greater than your yesterday.

I am rooting for you! Adios.

Regards

As I close this book, may all the realizations and lessons resonate upon your souls. Thank you for reaching this far, everyone. I hope soonest, you can be that better and great person the crowd didn't expect you to become.

Great skies my loves.

Sincerely,

Rjay Verdida

About the Author

Rjay Verdida

Rjay Verdida is a filipino-writer who typically writes romance fiction novels. He is 18-yrs-old and currently taking Bachelor of Science in Nursing in University of Rizal System-Taytay Campus.

He is a christian, wanderer, artist, and an avid fan of life. He sees the world in a different point of view, and that difference is his fuel to let his pen bleed to create more masterpieces that can change a being's life.

www.ingramcontent.com/pod-product-compliance
Lightning Source LLC
LaVergne TN
LVHW051512170726
843492LV00002B/895